Dedicated to children of all ages who have the courage to follow their heart.

Some days are full of sunshine. Everything stirs and grows and joyfully we dance and play to the music of our laughter. The light and warmth of the sun open up the world to us and we go out into life to explore, discover and experience. Happiness seems as natural and as certain as breathing. Yes, there are days like that but sometimes clouds gather in the clear blue sky, drawing together in a heavy layer to hide the face of the sun. Below, the world turns into a dull grey.

It was on such a day, when grey and heavy clouds covered most of the sky, that Teddy found himself on top of a small mound of rubbish and broken things. Blinking and shaking his head as though he was waking up from a bad dream, he sat up and looked around at the landfill site. It was a foreign and unfamiliar place, and the smell... he grimaced. How he found himself there he did not remember. All he could think of was that his owner had thrown him away with the words, 'You're no good anymore, too old and shabby.'

Teddy felt hurt at the memory and he just sat there with an empty look on his face. Out of the corner of his eye, he noticed a white butterfly joyfully fluttering around on its thin, delicate wings. Teddy wondered what it was doing in a place like this with nothing

but mounds of rubbish and broken things. It made him feel better to watch the butterfly and an almost-forgotten feeling of adventure arose in him.

'What do I really want?' Teddy asked himself. He knitted his brows trying hard to come up with an answer but the harder he tried the further away it seemed to be. He soon let go and, watching the butterfly, he forgot about everything else. It was then that the answer came to him, as light and effortless as the butterfly's flight: he wanted to be happy! Maybe, Teddy thought, a new friend would make me happy? Filled with new resolve, he got up, brushed off some of the dirt and climbed down. Standing firmly on the ground, he decided to look for a new friend.

Rat

Teddy had not been walking for long when a squeaky voice called him, 'Down here. I'm down here.' Teddy looked down in the direction of the voice and saw Rat with her head poking out of a hole in the ground.

Cautiously, Teddy moved closer. Rat scrabbled out and sat beside the hole fidgeting her long hairless tail between her paws. She pointed her snout in the direction of Teddy and twitched her whiskers trying to catch the scent of the newcomer.

'Who are you and what are you doing here?' Rat asked.

'I'm Teddy and I'm looking for a friend.' he answered, unsure what to make of her.

'A friend!' Rat squeaked, her eyes wandering all over Teddy. 'Ah, you look so soft and woolly inside...' and as she spoke, a dreamy expression crept over her face. Instinctively, Teddy took a few steps back. 'No, no! Don't go.' Rat pleaded, and her voice took on a honeyed tone. 'You see, I have a large family and many babies who would love to play in you... er, with you. You could have many new friends if you came with me down to my den.' Teddy stepped further away and, narrowing his eyes, took a good look at her. Teddy did not trust Rat, not an inch. Everything about her made him shiver all over and his fur stand on end: her squeaky voice, the small cunning eyes and especially the way she had looked at him before.

'I'm sorry, but I can't come with you. I'm too afraid of small dark places.' Teddy had never liked the dark and he clearly remembered being put, all alone, in a dark corner of the wardrobe when the new teddy bear had arrived. He had felt so afraid and alone…
Teddy shook his head trying to get rid of the horrible memory. He took a deep breath to brace himself and, without looking at her, he said goodbye and quickly walked away. Rat was calling to him making all sorts of promises but Teddy just kept on walking. All he wanted was to get as far away from her as possible. When he could no longer hear her, he dared to stop to catch his breath.

Magpie

Surrounded on all sides by rubbish and broken things, Teddy set out to explore some more still hoping to find a friend. He looked around and wondered where everything came from? With a few repairs, some of the broken things could still be useful. Just like me, he thought.

Teddy felt the hurt return and, if he had not run into Magpie, he might have given into the feeling once more. He stopped to watch the bird as it searched busily for something amongst the rubbish. 'What are you looking for?'

Magpie did not answer but eyed him with suspicion. Then her stare turned cold, 'This is my place.'

'Oh... But I don't want your place. I'm just looking for a friend.' Teddy said, trying to sound as assuring as possible.

'A friend...' Magpie mused, examining Teddy carefully. 'Friends aren't really that important if you ask me. No. Shiny things – they're important.' She no longer looked at Teddy, her gaze turning distant. 'I love shiny things... My home is full of the most amazing shiny things, so beautiful.'

'But... Maybe we could be friends? I could help you collect the shiny things you love so much.' Teddy suggested. Magpie looked at him and he thought he saw a little interest in her eyes.

'Hmmm... Do you like shiny things?'

'No, not really.' Teddy had to admit.

'You don't like shiny things!' she said with a frown. 'Well, then I don't think we could be friends. We are simply too different. Look at you, so shabby. You have nothing that shines. No, it would never work. You don't fit into my world. Just imagine what the other magpies would think if they saw us together!' Magpie puffed out her chest and flew away.

Gull

Once again, Teddy found himself alone. As he walked on, he wondered why appearance was so important to Magpie. He wanted to believe that it was the inside of someone that really mattered. Maybe he was wrong?

Teddy stopped and listened. Close by he could hear loud noises – a little too close for comfort. He took a few deep breaths to steady his nerves. Once calmer he walked ahead to find out what could possibly be causing it. As he came out from behind a small mound of rubbish, he saw two gulls fighting fiercely over a few scraps of food. Wings flapped, voices screeched and beaks pecked. Finally, one of the gulls succeeded in chasing the other away. Teddy kept his distance as the gull greedily began to eat. When it had finished, it noticed Teddy watching. 'Keehar! What are you looking at?' Gull asked.

'Nothing... I mean, you.' Hesitant, Teddy stepped a little closer, 'Why did you fight so hard? Why didn't you share?'

Gull looked at Teddy as though he had never heard anything quite so ridiculous, 'Gulls don't share. We never have, we never will. It's all about survival, being strong and taking what you can get.

Keehar! What are you doing here anyway?'

No longer so sure of himself, Teddy told Gull that he was looking for a friend.

'What's a friend?' Gull asked, puzzled.

'A friend... er... a friend is someone who cuddles you with a warm smile and tells you nice things when you most need it. Friends like to share with each other.'

'Gulls don't have friends. We have the flock. If you want to be part of the flock, you must be willing to fight for your food, even steal from the others. We only think of ourselves. It has always been that way. It cannot change. Keehar!' Gull screeched, leaving no room for discussion. Teddy so longed for a friend, longed to belong somewhere but the thought of living as Gull had just said made him feel so bad inside.

'I'm sorry,' Teddy said, 'I don't think I can live that way. It would be too hard for me.'

'I see...' Gull turned his head and with one of his little dark eyes took a closer look at Teddy. Then he poked Teddy's soft belly with his beak. 'Yes, you do look too soft and weak to be a gull. You don't have what it takes.' And with that he flew away.

Teddy stood for a little while rubbing his belly wondering why it was so hard to find a friend. Could there be something wrong with him? Maybe if he changed? If he became like others wanted him to be, maybe then?

Mouse Teddy continued his search amongst the rubbish and broken things but doubts had found their way into his head like little dark clouds keeping out the light and joy. Would he ever find a friend? Maybe an old teddy bear like him was not meant to be happy?

Maybe he should simply have stayed on the mound of rubbish and never gone out to look for a friend in the first place...

Lost in his worries, Teddy almost bumped into little Mouse. Mouse was wearing thick glasses and a green apron, and he was so busy weighing, measuring and sorting things into neat piles that he did not notice Teddy. Curious, Teddy asked Mouse what he was doing.

'Don't disturb me. Can't you see I'm busy! 10 grams, and the di-a-me-ter... This goes in the blue pile... I'm trying to find out what kind of place this is.'

'But...' Teddy looked around. 'But, it is a landfill!' He thought it was obvious.

'You never know,' Mouse said. 'Not until you have examined all the things, every single one. Oh, there is so much work to do, so much work.' He no longer took any notice of Teddy. Not knowing what else to do or where to go, Teddy remained where he was quietly watching Mouse work.

After a while Mouse looked up. 'You're still here?' he asked a little annoyed. 'Can't you see I'm working! What do you want?'

'I'm looking for a friend, but it seems so hard to find one here.'

'A friend! I don't have time for such things. I have much more important things to do.' He waved his paw impatiently as if to shoo Teddy away. Teddy would not be shooed away so easily. It might be his last chance to find a new friend.

'If I help you with your work, maybe you would have some time to be my friend?'

Mouse looked at Teddy with a thoughtful expression. He was not really interested in a friend but he needed help with his work and Teddy might be of use to him.

'Can you read and write?'

'No.' said Teddy.

'Well, can you count then?'

'I ... er ... count ...' Teddy knew what it meant to count - something with numbers - but he did not know how to. Afraid to let Mouse know, he hesitated, 'Count ... er ...'

'You aren't very clever, are you?' Mouse interrupted. 'I really don't see how we could possibly be friends. I'm much too clever for you. It would never work.' Teddy's heart sank at the harsh words.

'Maybe I could help you order and stack the things you have examined?' he said and reached out to stack some of the blue things. But in his eagerness to show that he could be useful, he hit one of the neat little piles. It tipped over into another pile and before long everything lay haphazardly on the ground.

'Oh, no! Look what you've done. So much work wasted.' Mouse looked angrily at

Teddy. 'You're not only stupid but you're also clumsy. Go away! Who would ever want to have a friend like you!'

Yes, Teddy thought, who would ever want to have a friend like me: an old and worn-out teddy bear of no use to anyone anymore. Slowly, Teddy turned around, and with heavy steps, left the landfill. He did not know where he was going. He no longer cared.

After some time, Teddy felt so tired in his short furry legs and lay down to rest on a small patch of grass by the side of the dusty path. He looked up at the sky and saw dark, heavy clouds that seemed to reach for each other like giants' big hands. He just lay there, watching, as the clouds drew shut, their dark, crooked fingers merged, blocking out the last rays of light and everything that was good and kind from his life. Teddy's eyes filled with tears. He cried and cried until he fell into a deep sleep.

Butterfly

'Teddy. Come on Teddy.' Teddy sat up and looked around. 'Come on Teddy! It's time to go.' The gentle voice belonged to a beautiful golden white butterfly resting on a flower beside him. With a sudden flutter, it took off, the wings shimmering in the sunlight.

Teddy struggled to his feet and followed it. 'Who are you, and where are we going?'

'I'm your guide on the journey you're about to begin.' Butterfly explained. 'I'm taking you to a special place, a magical garden. It's been waiting for you. You're ready now.'

'Waiting for me?' Teddy looked confused. 'But, why me? I'm just an old teddy bear. And why now?'

'Oh, so many questions. It's true then what they say about teddy bears.'

'What do they say?' Teddy wanted to know.

'Well, just that you're very curious little bears.' Teddy thought he heard it give a little laugh. 'Teddy, you're not "just" an old teddy bear, you're so much more.' With that, Butterfly flew ahead. She moved so fast that Teddy had to run to keep up with her. He enjoyed the feeling as he ran through the meadow. He felt he could run all day without getting tired.

In front of him Butterfly had stopped and, when Teddy caught up with her, his eyes opened wide with surprise.

As if from nowhere, a rainbow bridge had appeared. It was made of thousands of tiny lights in different colours. Teddy hesitated. 'Come on, Teddy. It's perfectly safe.' Butterfly said.

Teddy felt unsure but trusted her and very cautiously took a step onto the rainbow bridge. It felt soft, yet firm. Teddy took one more step and then another. As he walked across, the colours began to swirl and dance, flowing inside and all around him. Teddy enjoyed the feeling and, stepping onto the ground on the other side, he felt calm and light at heart.

The Magical Garden

Teddy looked around in wonder. In front of him lay a vast garden stretching out in all directions, further than his eyes could see. It was not like any ordinary garden. It seemed alive, radiant, and it glowed with a warm light welcoming him. 'Follow me.' Butterfly said and flew deeper into the garden. Sensing the garden felt safe, Teddy followed. Butterfly was right, he was a curious little bear.

They turned down a narrow path flanked by lovely flowers, their fragrance filling the air. Everywhere, Teddy could hear birdsong and the busy buzzing of bees as they skipped from flower to flower collecting sweet nectar. It was magical, just like the fairy tales he used to listen to.

Teddy paused beside a bed of beautiful roses, roses of all shapes, sizes and colours, even colours he had never seen before. He moved closer to one of the roses to smell its fragrance. It was then he heard the rose sing in a warm, tender voice. It sang to him of love and friendship. The song soothed him and his face softened. Reaching out his paw, he caressed the rose and thanked it for its song.

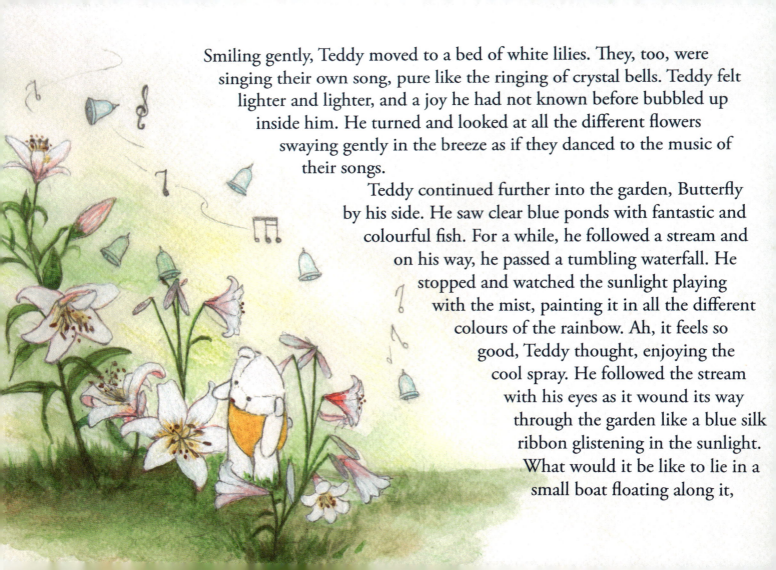

Smiling gently, Teddy moved to a bed of white lilies. They, too, were singing their own song, pure like the ringing of crystal bells. Teddy felt lighter and lighter, and a joy he had not known before bubbled up inside him. He turned and looked at all the different flowers swaying gently in the breeze as if they danced to the music of their songs.

Teddy continued further into the garden, Butterfly by his side. He saw clear blue ponds with fantastic and colourful fish. For a while, he followed a stream and on his way, he passed a tumbling waterfall. He stopped and watched the sunlight playing with the mist, painting it in all the different colours of the rainbow. Ah, it feels so good, Teddy thought, enjoying the cool spray. He followed the stream with his eyes as it wound its way through the garden like a blue silk ribbon glistening in the sunlight. What would it be like to lie in a small boat floating along it,

Teddy wondered?
Where would it
take me? To a lake with deep,
unexplored caves along the shore?
Or maybe even further, all the way to the sea?

An Enchanted Forest

A cluster of trees on the edge of a forest caught Teddy's attention and he left the river to explore. There were many different trees and they, too, were singing. Their songs were different from those of the flowers. He listened to the strong and bold beech, the old and wise oak and the tall and majestic cypress. Enchanted and a little overwhelmed by it all, Teddy stopped by a pine tree to rest. It was very calming to listen to the whispering wind as it passed through the pine needles.

Teddy sighed as he leaned against the tree and relaxed. He made his body still like a sturdy tree trunk and imagined roots growing from his toes, deep into the earth. The deeper they grew, the stronger and steadier he felt. He gently stretched imagining that he was growing taller and taller until he was the tallest tree in the garden. It felt so light and airy up there, full of space. Teddy had become like a mighty tree and soon he had forgotten all about time and even where he was…

Teddy became aware of his surroundings again by the gentle touch of Butterfly as she settled on his shoulder. 'Teddy! There is someone who wants to meet you.' Teddy stretched and wiggled his paws.

'Who is it?' he asked. Butterfly did not answer. She simply flew ahead to guide the way leading them deeper and deeper into the forest.

Teddy liked the cool dim lights and the way the streaks of sunlight shone through the treetops like golden fingers playfully caressing the forest floor. His eyes took in everything they saw. He listened to the deep songs of the tall trees and the sounds of the animals around him, many of which he had never heard before. Teddy noticed that the singing around him grew louder and more alive the further ahead they got, and he had a feeling they were moving towards the heart of the garden.

'Stop!' Butterfly whispered as they came round a sharp bend on the path. Teddy stopped, almost bumping into her.

'What is it?' he whispered back. Then he saw it, between the trees. It was the most beautiful creature Teddy had ever seen. There was something graceful and wild about it at the same time. It looked like a horse, only slightly bigger. It had soft silvery white hair, and the horn... In the middle of its forehead was a spiralling horn, gleaming as it caught a ray of sunlight. They stood, unmoving, looking at each other in silence. Then, as swiftly and quietly as it had appeared, it was gone, as if dissolving into the thicket. Teddy shook his head and blinked, 'Was it a... a unicorn?'

'Yes,' Butterfly said, 'It was a unicorn.'

'Will I ever see it again?' Teddy asked with deep longing in his voice.

'I don't know. Maybe. You were very fortunate to meet it.'

As they walked on, Teddy could not stop thinking about the unicorn. What would it be like riding on its back out on mysterious adventures? He could almost feel the wind on his face and body as they galloped across sunny meadows, through deep, unknown forests and over snow-capped mountains. What other strange and beautiful creatures would he meet?

Infront of them, the narrow forest path widened and the treetops began letting in more light. Teddy watched the sparkling play of light and shade and he was lost in wonder at the beauty of it all. Almost falling over his own two paws, Teddy clumsily came to a halt, his eyes wide open. At the end of one of the rays of light, a shining golden door had appeared. 'What is... how did it... where did it come from?' the words came tumbling out of him and he was quivering all over from excitement.

'It's The Door of Light. It's a magical door.' Butterfly answered calmly, not wanting to make Teddy more excited than he already was.

'But, what's behind it, where does it lead to?'

'Magical places – everything you can imagine, and more!' said Butterfly, 'And no, Teddy, it is not for now, another time and place. Someone is waiting for you, remember?'

'What do you mean... another place?' Teddy kept on. 'Can it change places or are there more than one?'

'No. There is only one but it can appear in different places at different times – it's magical!'

With no more words, Butterfly flew on ahead leaving The Door of Light behind and,

reluctantly, Teddy followed. He promised himself to find the door again, another time … and place, to find out what was behind it.

The Queen of the Garden

They soon left the coolness of the forest and stepped out into the warm sunshine. After a while, Butterfly stopped in front of a round lawn. Invited by the deep green colour of the grass, Teddy bent down and stroked it. It felt so soft and alive. Puzzled, Teddy watched as it rippled out to the sides just as when you throw a pebble into water.

In the centre of the lawn, there was a big crystal mirror, and on top of it a golden-white sphere of light shone like a little sun. The light was pure and it had a warm glow that made Teddy feel calm and peaceful. 'Welcome to my garden, Teddy.' said a melodious voice. At first, Teddy did not know where it came from. It was as though it came from everywhere at the same time. 'I am here, in the light.'

Teddy looked at the sphere of light in surprise, 'Who are you?'

'I'm known by many names but I prefer to call myself Queen of the Garden.' As she said her name, Teddy thought he could see an elegant, radiant Queen inside the sphere. 'I take care of all life in the garden,' she continued. 'The earth, the plants, the insects and all the animals. I give them each their song.'

'I didn't know that they could sing like that.' Teddy said.
'All life sings if you know how to listen. You have to be very quiet and listen with your heart, not your ears. The more you love someone the clearer his or her song will be.

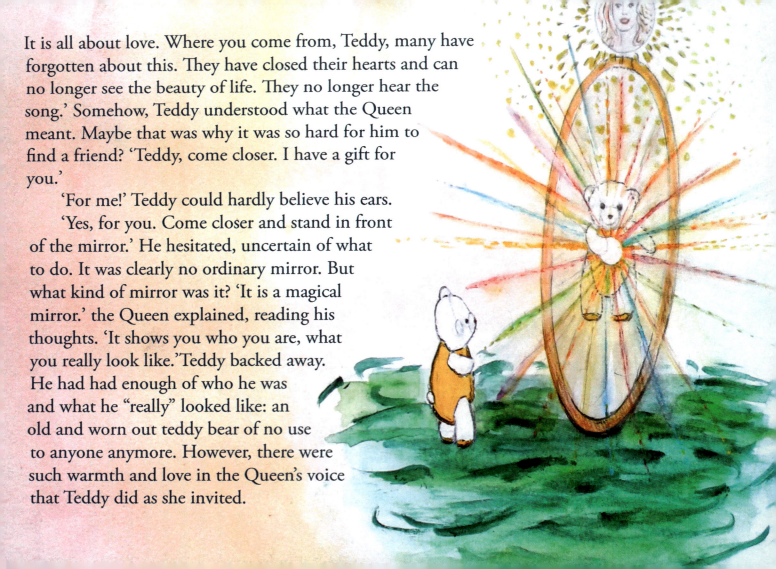

It is all about love. Where you come from, Teddy, many have forgotten about this. They have closed their hearts and can no longer see the beauty of life. They no longer hear the song.' Somehow, Teddy understood what the Queen meant. Maybe that was why it was so hard for him to find a friend? 'Teddy, come closer. I have a gift for you.'

'For me!' Teddy could hardly believe his ears.

'Yes, for you. Come closer and stand in front of the mirror.' He hesitated, uncertain of what to do. It was clearly no ordinary mirror. But what kind of mirror was it? 'It is a magical mirror.' the Queen explained, reading his thoughts. 'It shows you who you are, what you really look like.' Teddy backed away. He had had enough of who he was and what he "really" looked like: an old and worn out teddy bear of no use to anyone anymore. However, there were such warmth and love in the Queen's voice that Teddy did as she invited.

To his surprise there was no reflection, just an empty space. 'Open your heart, Teddy. Relax, and trust in yourself.' the Queen said with a calm voice, and because she seemed to have no doubt that he could, he did. It was then that he saw his reflection in the mirror. He noticed a tiny light, like a shining seed, that seemed to come from within his heart. The more he opened his heart and the more he trusted in himself, the brighter the light shone. Instead of an old worn-out teddy bear, he saw a beautiful shining one. He felt so full of love, happy and content with whom he was. He now knew that although he had an old teddy bear body, it was not who he really was.

'I AM beautiful...' he said softly.

The Queen looked at Teddy with love, 'Yes, you are beautiful – you are perfect just being you!' The Queen paused. It was a lot for a teddy bear to take in and the Queen had not finished, 'When you leave the garden, you will forget what you have just seen. However, the seed of light will remain with you in your heart. You must take care of it and nurture it with thoughts and feelings of love and kindness towards yourself and others. When you help someone, the seed will grow and shine brighter and, when the time is right, you will discover your own song.

Teddy frowned. Why would the Queen say something like that? How could he possibly forget what he had just seen? No! He would never forget, and he would never leave the garden where he felt so good. Besides, there were so many things he still wanted to explore.

'You are tired and need to rest.' the Queen said interrupting his thoughts. She was right. All the new things that had happened to him had made him very tired and he had a wobbly feeling in his body. Even though he still had questions he wanted to ask, he lay down sinking deep into the soft green grass.

He cast a last loving look at the Queen and Butterfly. 'Thank you, thank you – for everything.' he said and fell asleep.

A New Beginning

When Teddy woke up, he was lying on the small patch of grass by the side of the road. The sun was shining, soaking into his body, warming him. He felt relaxed lying there in the soft grass but also a bit strange, as if something had happened to him. It was like a hazy and far away dream.

Teddy stayed very still for a while listening to the sounds around him: the bees buzzing near the flowers, the birdsong and the rustling leaves as the wind passed through the trees. He felt good as he stretched his body and rubbed the sleep from his eyes. By his side a butterfly rested peacefully, slowly opening and closing its wings. It looked familiar to him, as though he had seen it before in some other place. He felt such love and respect for everything he saw, including himself. It was a new and unexpected feeling.

All Teddy could think of was to share his newfound joy and happiness with someone, just like the sun shares its warmth and light with all life on earth. The mere thought of giving and sharing made him feel happy.

'Mummy, mummy! Look, a teddy bear.' a young girl, who was walking with her mother, had seen Teddy lying there in the sun. 'Can I take him home? I think he would like a friend. Can I?'

'I don't see why not,' the mother replied. 'It looks like someone has thrown him away, like they don't want him anymore.'

The girl gently picked Teddy up, cuddled him, and with a warm smile she said, 'I'll call you Teddy Sunshine because that is where I found you, in the sunshine.'

A Song

As they walked away, a little playful note found its way into Teddy's head. At first, it was faint and alone. Then other, different sounds came along and began to play with each other. Their joyful play formed a melody, and quietly Teddy began humming a little song he remembered from long ago – a song as old as time...

In the beginning, the darkness of night
The Singer lay resting, dreaming of light.
Inside Her womb, sounds took on form
A song, like a child, waiting to be born.

Gently She moved, She had an idea
She wanted to know Her song, to hear.
Clearing Her throat, she began to hum
To sing little notes of light, it was fun.

Sounds flowed forth, bounced off the wall
Returned to the Singer in Her great hall.
She liked what She heard and wanted more
She sang and sang, Her throat a little sore.

The song was simple and full of light
It swirled and danced, twinkled in the night.
Each bright note had a life of its own
Growing, unfolding like a seed that's sown.

Some notes were joyful, delicate and pure
Others more serious, so deep and sure.
Some notes were wilful, strong with might
Others more gentle, with warmth and delight.

She sang of heaven, of sun and star
She sang of living and who we are.
She sang of the earth and life thereon
Of playing and learning in loving fun.

About the Author

Michael Voss Grangaard is an experienced storyteller for children. He is a pedagogue and teacher, specializing in religious studies and philosophy, and uses storytelling as a means of facilitating philosophical conversations with children. He has been invited to give talks to fellow teachers on this subject by the educational branch of the Danish National Church. He has studied and practiced extensively within different spiritual traditions from the East and West and draws on his own insights and experiences when writing and telling stories.

Michael has also trained as a mindfulness teacher for children aged 4-19, and works with individuals, smaller groups and classes in schools in the United Kingdom, where he lives. In his work with children, he uses a heart-to-heart approach creating a space where it is safe to explore life as it unfolds inside and outside ourselves. He teaches simple tools for children to handle difficult thoughts and feelings and points the way towards a life based in kindness.

For information on Michael's work, please e-mail michaelvg1@outlook.com

About the Illustrator and Designer

Ilona Pimbert has always been attracted to art from a very young age and drawing in particular has been her most confident and natural way of expressing herself. She studied Fine Art at Chelsea College of Art and Central Saint Martins School of Art at the University of London in the United Kingdom, and she now works as a freelance artist.

Ilona strongly believes that imagination and empathy for the world are truly powerful in healing people and helping us to fully grow into whole human beings. This idea underpins her work and continues to inspire her as an artist.

For information on Ilona's art and work, please go to www.talesofcolour.com
or email ilona@talesofcolour.com

Made in the USA
Charleston, SC
27 February 2016